Friends to the Rescue

by Justine Korman and Ron Fontes

Random House New York
Copyright © 1998 Universal Studios Publishing Rights,
a division of Universal Studios Licensing, Inc.
Babe, Babe:Pig in the City, Babe and Friends, and all related characters
are copyrights and trademarks of Universal City Studios, Inc.
Licensed by Universal Studios Licensing, Inc.
All rights reserved under International and Pan-American Copyright Conventions.
Published in the United States by Random House, Inc., New York, and
simultaneously in Canada by Random House of Canada Limited, Toronto.
Library of Congress Catalog Card Number: 98-66063
www.randomhouse.com/kids
ISBN: 0-679-89456-X
Printed in the United States of America 10 9 8 7 6 5 4 3 2 1

When Babe and the Boss's wife, Mrs. Hoggett, went off to the state fair, Ferdinand decided to follow them. After all, Babe was his best friend!

But when he reached the city, Ferdinand didn't know where to start looking.

Just then, he heard a familiar song—**"La, la, la!"**

Sure enough, it was Babe. He and his new city friends were singing because Zootie the chimp had just had twins.

Ferdinand was thrilled to find his friend at the Flealands Hotel. "Give us a peck," he said to Babe. "I'm with my lucky Pig—safe at last!"

But the authorities had also heard the animals' happy song. Like Ferdinand, they had followed the sound of the singing until they found the hotel. Then they burst through the doors with nets and muzzles. The animals all ran.

Ferdinand hid under a lampshade. Then Babe nearly got caught, but Ferdinand came to his rescue. Many other animals were not so lucky.

The captured animals were loaded into a van. Babe's friend
Flealick, a little dog on wheels, tried to stop the van. Babe,
Ferdinand, and a monkey named Tug nervously watched as
Flealick almost got squashed!

Babe, Ferdinand, and Tug ran to help Flealick.

"Flip me over," the little dog barked weakly.

He sniffed the air. "They went this-a-way," he said, pointing with his nose.

Babe sniffed the air, too. Until now, he had used his nose only to find food. Now he realized his snout could find friends as well.

"Actually, Flealick, I think it's...**that** way," said Babe, pointing in a different direction.

Babe's nose led them all over the city.
Finally, they reached a big building. Babe's little snout told him that they had found their kidnapped friends.

Tug climbed up to a window and peeked in. He saw their friends locked up in cages. He motioned down to Babe and Flealick.

"Let's go get 'em!" Flealick barked.

"Wait," said Babe. "If we get caught, we won't be able to help anybody."

Flealick stayed under the stairs as a lookout while Babe, Ferdinand, and Tug sneaked up to the room where their friends were. They hid behind the door, waiting for the workers to leave.

Finally, the last worker left.
Tug opened the door.
"Hello? Hello?" Babe called into the dim room full of cages.
The animals were so happy to see Babe. "I knew he'd come!" said a pink poodle.

Babe, Ferdinand, and Tug let the animals out of their cages. "May I suggest that we stay calm, maintain a tight formation, and proceed in an orderly fashion," said Babe.

"And may he suggest that we do it **real fast!**" Ferdinand added.

Meanwhile, down below, Flealick was watching anxiously as one of the technicians returned and headed back up the stairs!

The animals in the lab hid when they heard the sound of footsteps outside the door.

Then they heard a click as the door was locked. They were trapped!

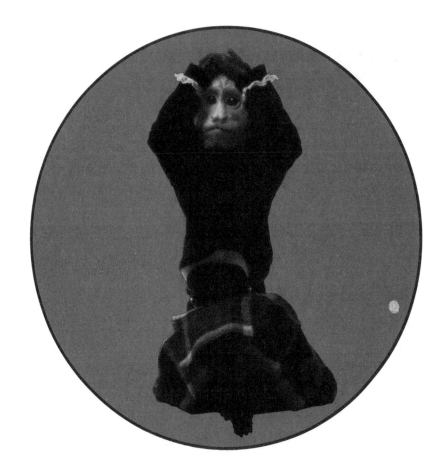

The animals quickly came up with a plan. Together, they built a tower of cages, boxes, stools, and chairs leading up to a hole in the ceiling. The animals climbed the tower to the ceiling. From there Babe led his friends through a pipe to the hospital next door.

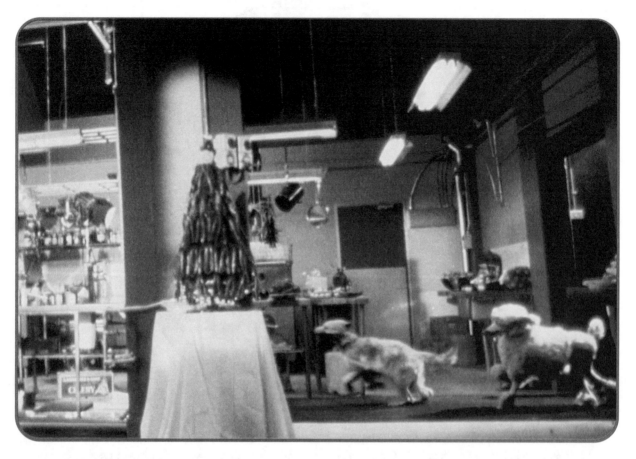

The friends walked through the children's ward. One little boy watched the fantastic parade go by. Then he smiled and fell back asleep.

The animals took an elevator down to the ground floor— right to the hospital kitchen!

The chef was so surprised that he dropped his pots. The animals ran, and the chef chased after them.

They ran through a door—and found themselves in the
middle of a giant banquet! Luckily, the animals spotted Babe's
human, Mrs. Hoggett. She was wearing a clown suit. She saw
Babe, too. "I'm Esme Cordelia Hoggett and I've come for my
Arthur's pig!" she screamed.

She scooped Babe up in her arms. At last he was safe!

But the excitement wasn't over yet. The chimp family had hidden in the chandelier. Just as it was about to fall, they all jumped off—all except one of the babies!

"Thelonius!" squealed Babe to the tall orangutan.

Thelonius looked up just in time to catch the falling baby!

After their exciting adventures, the animals were ready to get out of the city. Luckily, Babe had the perfect place for them all—Hoggett Farm!